SHADOW PLAY

SHADOW

BY **Penny Harter**

ILLUSTRATED BY **Jeffrey Greene**

PLAY

Night Haiku

SIMON & SCHUSTER BOOKS FOR YOUNG READERS
Published by Simon & Schuster
New York London Toronto Sydney Tokyo Singapore

SIMON & SCHUSTER BOOKS FOR YOUNG READERS
1230 Avenue of the Americas, New York, New York 10020
Text copyright © 1994 by Penny Harter. Illustrations copyright © 1994 by Jeffrey Greene.
SIMON & SCHUSTER BOOKS FOR YOUNG READERS
is a trademark of Simon & Schuster. Designed by Paul Zakris.
The text for this book is set in 23-point Gill Sans. The illustrations were done in pastels.
Manufactured in the United States of America
10 9 8 7 6 5 4 3 2 1

Library of Congress Cataloging-in-Publication Data
Harter, Penny.   Shadow play, night haiku / by Penny Harter ;
illustrated by Jeffrey Greene.   p. cm.
Summary: A collection of haiku devoted to night related themes.
1. Night—Juvenile poetry.   2. Children's poetry, American.   3. Haiku, American.
[1. Night—Poetry.   2. American poetry—Collections.   3. Haiku.]
I. Greene, Jeffrey, ill. II. Title.
PS3558.A6848S48   1994 811'.54—dc20   93-39887   CIP AC
ISBN: 0-671-88396-8

For Charlie and Nancy
—P . H .

For Ross, Aedwyn, Jacquie, Allan, and Bob
—J . G .

ACKNOWLEDGMENTS

"out the train window," "only letting in the cat," "mountain thunder," "all night rain...," and "distant streetlights" from *The Orange Balloon,* published by From Here Press, copyright © 1980 by Penny Harter. Reprinted by permission of the author.

"shooting star" from *From the Willow,* published by Wind Chimes Press, copyright © 1983 by Penny Harter. Reprinted by permission of the author.

"full moon—/light in the cracks," "the monkey's face," "distant thunder," "dew falling," "nightfall—," "closed bedroom door," and "snow finished" from *The Monkey's Face,* published by From Here Press, copyright © 1987 by Penny Harter. Reprinted by permission of the author.

"at dusk a cloud," "moonless night," "deep in the pine," "before sleep," "evening rain—," "through the telescope," "the snowman's smile," "in the tunnel," and "midnight sirens" from *Stages and Views,* published by Katydid Books, copyright © 1994 by Penny Harter. Reprinted by permission of the author.

mountain thunder
lightning
between the stars

evening rain—
in the foam of the waterfall
white petals

before sleep
I open the window
to let in the rain

in the dark kitchen
the open refrigerator door
swings shut

far away, the sound
of running water...
I snuggle deeper

in the tunnel
of the bed, my feet
so far away

a train whistle...
far down the tracks
the red light

railroad crossing...
the long glint
of the moon

out the train window
the night trees
darker than the sky

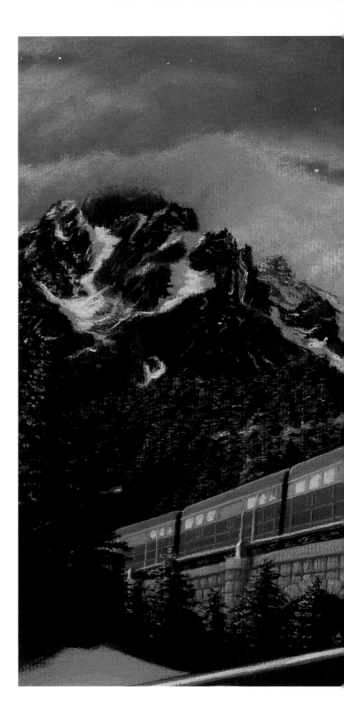

through the telescope
the mountains on the moon—
Grandmother yawns

lunar eclipse—the shadow
moves on the watcher's
upturned face

midnight sirens—
three dogs howl
in harmony

distant thunder—
overhead a satellite
moves in the dark

country road—
all the stars pour through
the car radio

by the roadside
one cow lifts her face
into our headlights

all night long
light shines in the eyes
of the carousel ponies

the fortuneteller
traces the line in my palm
to a star

whistling, whistling
fireworks follow one another
into the night

only letting in the cat
until
the morning star

the cat wakes me up
chasing his tail
in the dark

all night rain...
on the bed, the cat
licks his fur

across my bed
flickers from the television
and moonlight

the monkey's face
between my hands—
winter twilight

all night storm...
my room fills with
snow light

deep in the pine
the deserted nest—
evening breeze

moonless night...
as many crickets singing
as the stars

at dusk a cloud
of fireflies rises—
the Milky Way

nightfall—
the coolness of dirt
between toes

dew falling
on the clothesline
a towel glimmers

out after dark...
chasing flashlight circles
across the grass

shooting star...
the river
still frozen

full moon—
light in the cracks
of the sidewalk

the snowman's smile
melts in the moonlight—
spring thaw

snow finished—
the blaze
of winter stars

out the plane window
all those headlights
going somewhere

distant streetlights—
constellations
moving past

floorboards creak—
down the hall, a light
goes on, goes off

closed bedroom door—
her shadow darkens
the crack of light

on my wall
two monsters fight—
shadow play